Patti, have you gone crazy?

"Cut it out, Wayne Miller!" I yelled, without even bothering to turn around. Wayne Miller is this awful guy.

"They're reading the Winter Carnival poster, Wayne," his creepy little friend, Ronny Wallace, reported with a snicker.

"Let them look," Wayne said. "We're going to win all the prizes. Girls never win anything anyway!"

"Oh, yeah, Wayne?" Patti stopped and glared at him. "I am so totally convinced you're wrong that I'll . . . I'll personally do your next science project for you if *we* don't win more contests than *you* do at the Winter Carnival!"

"You got a deal!" Wayne stuck out his hand. "Shake!"

"Shake!" Patti grabbed it and shook, hard.

Kate groaned. "Patti, have you gone crazy?"

Look for these and other books
in the Sleepover Friends Series:

SLEEPOVER FRIENDS

Patti Gets Even

Susan Saunders

AN
APPLE
PAPERBACK

SCHOLASTIC INC.
New York Toronto London Auckland Sydney

ISBN 0-590-42367-3

12 11 10 9 8 7 6 5 4 3 2 1   8 9/8 0 1 2 3/9

Printed in the U.S.A.   28

First Scholastic printing, October 1989

Chapter
1

"So . . . what's the big surprise?" Stephanie Green asked Patti Jenkins.

"You'll see," Patti said. She sounded really excited. "Okay — stand back."

"Stand back?" Kate Beekman said. "Did you lend her Bullwinkle for the day, Lauren?"

Kate was talking to me — I'm Lauren Hunter. Bullwinkle is my family's dog, who can knock you down in three seconds flat. The four of us — Stephanie, Patti, Kate, and I — were at Patti's house, standing at the door to Mr. Jenkins's study. Patti reached dramatically for the doorknob.

"No, it's not a pet," she said with a grin. "At least, not exactly. Close your eyes."

"Come onnnnn!" Stephanie complained. "We're starving."

Kate and I nodded in agreement. My brother, Roger, was waiting outside for us in his car. He'd promised to drive us to the mall for a pizza-to-go as soon as we'd picked up Patti.

But Patti insisted. "Come on you guys . . . please?"

"All right. . . ." Kate and Stephanie squeezed their eyes shut. I did, too.

I heard Patti turn the knob on the study door. For a second everything was quiet. Then suddenly I heard all these whirring and clicking sounds.

"You can open your eyes now," Patti said.

I opened mine and blinked twice. "Wow!" I said.

"What is it?" Stephanie cried.

"It's a robot!" Kate exclaimed.

In front of us was a small, silver, mechanical man. Actually, the robot didn't look all that much like a man. He didn't have separate legs for one thing. For another, his feet were little treads, smaller versions of the ones you see on bulldozers. He didn't have eyes either, and his ears were dish-shaped antennas. But he did have a head, and two arms that looked sort of like Slinkys with funny round hands that had three metal fingers apiece.

"This is Oddjob," Patti said with a proud smile.

"Where did you get him?" Kate asked.

"Does he talk?" asked Stephanie.

"What can he do?" I wanted to know.

"He belongs to my Uncle Nick," Patti said, answering Kate's question.

"Your mom's brother, the one who's an engineer in California?" asked Kate.

"He's the one," Patti replied. "He's going to be working on a computer project in Europe for six months so he left Oddjob with us!"

"What can Oddjob do?" I asked again.

He wasn't doing anything right then. He was just standing in the middle of the floor, not moving at all. Somewhere inside his round metal body the whirring and clicking were still going on.

"Just what his name says," Patti told me. "Chores around the house, like vacuuming, mopping, and dusting. He can even saw wood."

"He *cleans*?" I said in an astonished voice. "I could sure use a robot like that!"

3

"Or two or three," Kate teased. I'm not what you'd call especially neat. In fact, my room is usually a disaster area.

"How does he work?" Stephanie asked Patti. "Do you just say, Oddjob, clean the house, and he does it? It sounds like magic!"

Kate snorted. "He's a robot, not a genie, Stephanie," she said.

"He's not quite that advanced," Patti admitted. "But he's pretty amazing. Uncle Nick says he's a state-of-the-art robot, and that means he's about as advanced as robots get. He'll respond to certain voices — my uncle's, of course, and my mom's. Uncle Nick just programmed him to obey me, too. But voice commands have to be one word only, or he gets confused. Like *Vacuum* or — "

She was interrupted by an extra-loud whir. "Vacuum!" a tinny voice repeated. Holding out his right hand, Oddjob came rolling toward Patti.

"Cancel. Cancel!" she said quickly. The robot lurched to a stop.

"I'll have to be careful what I say in front of him," Patti said with a giggle. "There's also a remote control for more complicated orders . . . I'll show you."

4

She hurried into the study. Then she came right back out, frowning. "Horace!" she yelled. Horace is Patti's little brother. He is only in first grade, but as far as I can tell his brain has already gone to college! "Hor-rrrace! I'm telling Mom. . . ."

"What do you want?" a muffled voice called out.

"I don't believe it. He's hiding in the closet!" Patti darted back into the study. She quickly reappeared, dragging Horace behind her. Horace is a skinny little kid with big front teeth and brown hair that sticks up all over the place.

"I was just trying out a couple of Oddjob's programs," Horace protested. That might sound like a funny thing for a first-grader to say, but then you don't know Horace. I'll bet he learned how to program a computer before he'd even learned how to walk!

But Patti took the remote control box out of his hands. It was about the size of a TV remote, but it looked like a computer keyboard. "This is not a toy," she scolded. "Mom told you to stay away from Oddjob unless one of us was with you!"

Horace made a face.

Outside a horn beeped three times.

"That's Roger," I said. "If we don't hurry up . . ."

"Okay. We have six whole months to fool around with Oddjob." Patti pressed a couple of buttons on the remote control box. Oddjob clicked into reverse and backed into the study.

"Let me just grab my overnight stuff," Patti said, closing the door on the robot. "Remember what Mom told you, Horace!" She pointed a warning finger at her little brother, and raced upstairs. In a flash, she came back down again wearing her coat and scarf and carrying her tote.

"Good night, Mom," she called out. "See you tomorrow."

"Good night, girls." Mrs. Jenkins waved from the living room. We headed out the front door.

"What did you do with the remote?" I asked Patti as we piled into Roger's old green car.

"I hid it in my room," Patti answered. "Siblings are impossible!" she added, meaning Horace.

"You said it!" Roger muttered from behind the wheel.

"Poor Roger," said Stephanie, grinning at him as she climbed into the front seat. "And you not only have Lauren to deal with, you have the three of us, too.''

Roger sighed, and nodded sadly.

''You don't get credit for *always* having to put up with the four of us, though,'' Kate pointed out.

''That's right,'' I said. In the beginning it was just Kate and me.

Kate and I are practically next-door neighbors on Pine Street. There's just one house between us. We started playing together when we were babies.

By kindergarten, we were best friends. That's when the sleepovers started. Every Friday night, either Kate would sleep over at my house, or I would sleep over at hers.

We played grown-up and school. We made s'mores in the toaster oven and filled the freezers with cherry Kool Pops. And we started watching movies on TV.

Kate's a real movie freak. Musicals, foreign films, sci-fi — you name it, she'll watch it. She'd like to be a movie director someday. So, as we got older, movies were the one thing we didn't give up.

7

Whatever we were doing, it was always just Kate and me.

Then, the summer before fourth grade, Stephanie Green moved to Riverhurst from the city. She and I ended up in the same fourth-grade class, 4A, which is how we got to know each other.

Stephanie could do all the latest dance steps. She already had her own style of dressing, too — like always wearing red, black, and white, to go with her dark hair. I thought she was great. I wanted Kate to get to know her as well. I figured Kate would like her as much as I did. But it didn't work out that way.

Instead, it was hate-at-first-sight, or at least instant dislike! Kate thought Stephanie was an airhead. "All she cares about is shopping," she said. Stephanie thought Kate was a stuffy know-it-all. Roger said the problem was obvious. "They're too much alike — both bossy."

But I didn't give up. I invited Stephanie to a Friday sleepover at my house. Then she invited me *and* Kate (after I insisted) to one at her house. Finally Kate asked Stephanie to one of *her* sleepovers. Little by little, the Sleepover Twins became a trio.

Not that Kate and Stephanie suddenly got along.

They still argued like crazy about a lot of things, and I usually found myself caught in the middle. Then Patti Jenkins moved to Riverhurst.

Patti's from the city, too, but she's as quiet and shy as Stephanie is bubbly and outgoing. She and Stephanie had gone to the same school, and Stephanie wanted Patti to be part of our gang. "She'll even things out," was how Stephanie put it.

Kate and I both liked Patti right away. She's kind and thoughtful, not to mention one of the smartest kids at Riverhurst Elementary. Besides that, she's the only girl in fifth grade who's taller than I am! So school had barely started this year, and we'd collected a *fourth* Sleepover Friend!

Roger was turning into the mall parking lot. He looked down at his watch. "It is now six-seventeen. You have exactly fifteen minutes. If you're not back here by six thirty-two on the nose, I'm going to — "

"I know, I know," I interrupted. "If we're not back here by six thirty-two, you're going to leave us high and dry because you have a date with Linda at seven. Then we'll have to walk home in all this snow, and we'll probably freeze to death."

"I want some Rocky Road from Sweet Stuff," Stephanie was saying. Sweet Stuff is the best candy store in town. "And if we have any time left over, we can dash past Just Juniors. . . ."

"Let's scramble!" said Kate, and the four of us practically fell out of the car.

10

Chapter 2

"Hurry! We've probably already used up forty-five seconds!" Stephanie cried as we skidded across the frozen parking lot. "Brrr! I *hate* this weather!"

It was so cold my teeth were chattering.

"At least w-we have the W-winter Carnival to l-look forward t-to next w-weekend," I said.

For three days every year, Riverhurst celebrates winter with a big carnival. They always have a huge bonfire, fireworks, ice-skating on Munn's Pond, a band concert, sleigh rides, and best of all, lots of good food.

"Not to mention your new brother or sister, Stephanie," Kate added. Mrs. Green was expecting

11

a baby, and it was due sometime in the next two weeks.

"Aren't you getting excited?" Patti asked.

The four of us shot through the sliding glass doors into the warm mall.

Stephanie pulled off her red-and-white wool cap and her black mittens. "I don't know . . . ," she answered slowly. "You guys haven't made the idea seem all that attractive."

Stephanie had spent eleven years as the only child in the Green family. As Kate and Patti and I had been telling her for months, she was in for a serious shock.

"But *babies* aren't bad," Patti said soothingly, brushing snowflakes out of her hair. "They're cuddly and they smile a lot. Since they can't walk, or even crawl, they can't really get into trouble. When they cry, you just feed them and they stop right away. Actually, babies are kind of sweet."

"But what about when they get older?" Kate said grimly.

We call Kate's little sister Melissa the Monster, which should give you some idea of how *she's* turning out.

"Have you come up with any new names?" Patti asked.

We turned up the main aisle of the mall toward the Pizza Palace.

Stephanie shrugged. "Vanessa if it's a girl, Cedric if it's a boy," she said.

"Cedric?" Kate repeated, raising an eyebrow.

"Yeah, my parents weren't wild about it, either," Stephanie said. "What do you think of *Sting*?"

"Sting Green," Kate said. "Now, that has a real ring to it!"

All of us giggled.

"We have to start picking out a baby gift," Patti reminded us.

"I think everything's been taken care of already," Stephanie said. "Nana" — that's what Stephanie calls her grandmother, Mrs. Bricker — "bought the crib and a chest of drawers to match. Aunt Janet sent all the sheets and blankets a baby could ever use! Mr. and Mrs. Blake sent a huge stuffed panda. Mr. Binder gave us a playpen, and Mr. and Mrs. Rosten sent a stroller." Stephanie's dad is a lawyer at Blake, Binder, and Rosten.

"Look at that," Patti exclaimed, screeching to a

halt in front of a new store called Baby Boom. "I'll bet the baby hasn't gotten one of those!" She pointed at the window.

"Is that cute?" I said.

"It's perfect," Kate agreed.

"Good for a boy *or* girl," Patti pointed out.

The brightly lit window was crowded with tiny striped jumpsuits, pajamas dotted with blue and yellow ducks, frilly little dresses, and a big stuffed gold half-moon on a string. Right in the center was a denim jacket absolutely covered with satin patches, embroidery, and silver studs. I would have gladly worn it myself, but it was about the size of Stephanie's wool cap.

"It's darling!" Stephanie said. "Let's take a quick look." She tried the door of Baby Boom and shook her head. "It's locked. The store must close at six."

"That's okay. I can read the price tag if I turn my head sideways . . . ," I said. I squinted and pressed my face against the glass. "Sixty-eight dollars!"

"For something that small?" Kate turned her head sideways to see for herself.

But Stephanie nodded wisely. "I'll bet it's imported. Forget it, you guys."

14

" 'Sponsor of the Winter Carnival,' " Patti read from a sign at the bottom of the Baby Boom window. "I wonder what that means?"

Stephanie and I shrugged. Kate looked at her watch. "Come on!" she said. "We only have eleven minutes to order pizza, have John cook it, buy everything else we want to eat, and — "

"Okay, okay," said Stephanie, speeding up.

"Patti, you and Lauren go to the Pizza Palace," Kate said. "I'll go with Stephanie to make sure she doesn't buy out Sweet Stuff!"

"Do we want the usual?" I asked. The usual is a king-size double-cheese pizza with pepperoni and mushrooms.

Stephanie nodded. "We'll pick up some Rocky Road and what else?" she asked.

"Chocolate bark?" Patti suggested.

"Or chocolate-covered cherries," I added.

"Fine. We'll meet you in five." Stephanie and Kate made a quick right turn into Sweet Stuff.

Patti and I hurried into the Pizza Palace, which was across the main aisle.

The Pizza Palace is about as far from a palace as you can imagine. It's a small place with four video games near the front door, a long counter with stools

15

to one side, and a big, black pizza oven at the back. But even though it's definitely no palace, it still has the best pizza in town.

John, the cook, was standing behind the counter, serving slices to two older men. "Hello, girls," he said when he saw Patti and me. "The usual?"

We nodded. "And could you hurry, please, John?" I asked. "I'm afraid we're in kind of a rush. . . ."

John nodded and quickly started spreading tomato sauce and cheese on an unbaked crust. Meanwhile Patti and I looked over the posters and notices beside the front door. One of them announced a Bingo game at the Elks Lodge. Another advertised a garage sale on Glendale. I was checking out what they'd be selling when Patti said, "Look, Lauren, here's something else about the carnival!"

"Let me see." I moved over to read the poster. "This year the Winter Carnival will have the following contests with trophies for the winners: a dogsled race to Munn's Pond, a snow sculpture contest for twelves and under, ice-dancing, a snow maiden contest. . . ."

"And check this out!" Patti said, pointing at the bottom. "The sponsors of the carnival give prizes

16

from their stores to the winners, too," she turned to me. "Baby Boom is a sponsor," she said. "Maybe we can *win* that jacket for the baby!"

"By doing what?" I looked over the list of contests again. I was trying to figure out if there was even *one* we might have a chance at, when suddenly there was a tremendous burp, right in my ear!

"Cut it out, Wayne Miller!" I yelled without even bothering to turn around. Wayne Miller is this awful guy in Mrs. Milton's class, 5A, and I'd know one of his burps anywhere!

"They're reading the Winter Carnival poster, Wayne," his creepy little friend, Ronny Wallace, reported with a snicker. Ronny has been Wayne's sidekick for as long as anyone can remember. It's a good thing they like each other because no one else can stand either one of them.

"Let them look," Wayne said. "We're going to win them all anyway."

"Oh, really?" I asked politely. "Like you won the bike race?" I turned around and stared into his small brown eyes. Wayne was in the Riverhurst bike-a-thon last fall, and he went around telling everyone he was sure to win it. But Kate, Stephanie, and I beat him — even though he *cheated* to win!

Wayne glared at me.

"Are you going to be the Snow Maiden, Wayne?" Patti put in sweetly.

Patti almost never says anything mean to anyone, but even *she* can't stand Wayne Miller.

Ronny started snickering again, but Wayne stopped him with a look. "No, not the *snow maiden contest*," he said, talking in a high voice to imitate Patti. "I'm entering the dogsled race, the snow sculpture contest — "

"Since when have you been interested in art, Wayne?" Kate asked. She and Stephanie had just walked through the door of the Pizza Palace with a large box from Sweet Stuff.

Wayne snorted. "Who said anything about *art*? We're gonna build a big snow fort, with snow cannons and tanks!"

Kate rolled her eyes. "I should have known," she said.

"And I guess you think you'll win the dogsled race with Killer," I said. Killer is Wayne's dog. He is the same size as Bullwinkle, but much meaner and uglier!

"You got it," Wayne replied. "I've trained him

to pull my sled and everything. Killer's a true champion, not like that useless mutt of yours."

"What did you say?!" I squawked. "Who are you calling a *useless mutt*?"

"For your information, Wayne Miller," Patti said loudly, "Bullwinkle's twice as much a champion as Killer could ever be!"

"How would you know?" Wayne said with a sneer. "When would you have had any time to see Killer race? You're too busy hanging out with those egghead wimps and weirdos. . . ."

He meant the Quarks Club, an after-school science club Patti belongs to, along with some other kids at Riverhurst Elementary.

"Watch what you say about my friend, Wayne Miller!" Stephanie yelled. She always jumps right into arguments, and she's good at them, too. Maybe because her father is a lawyer and is always encouraging her to learn how to state her case.

"Hey!" John called from behind the counter. "Don't deafen my customers. Your pizza's ready," he added with a grin, looking at us.

He frowned at Wayne and Ronny. "Do you two want to order? Or are you just hanging around, causing trouble?"

"We're going to play some video games," Wayne answered quickly. He dropped a quarter into Alien Attackers and hunched over the screen.

I paid for our pizza and picked up the box. Kate, Patti, Stephanie, and I started for the door. But when we passed Wayne, he muttered just loud enough for us to hear, "Why do I even bother to argue? Girls never win anything anyway!"

"Oh, yeah, Wayne?" Patti stopped and glared at him. She was still mad about his Quarks remark. She's pretty sensitive about being thought of as an egghead. "I am so totally convinced that you're wrong, that I'll . . . I'll personally do your next science project for you if we don't win more contests than you do at the Winter Carnival!" Patti was calm — almost too calm. And her voice was low and serious. I'd never seen her so mad!

"You got a deal!" Wayne stuck out his hand. "Shake!"

"Shake!" Patti grabbed it and shook hard.

Kate groaned and looked at her watch. "Six-thirty," she wailed. "Come on, you guys. We've got to get out of here!"

Chapter
3

"Patti, have you gone crazy?" Kate hissed as the four of us rushed through the mall toward the doors to the parking lot. "You're usually so sensible."

"You could get into big trouble, doing a science project for Wayne Miller," I added. I couldn't believe Patti was serious about our entering any contests at the Winter Carnival.

"I'm *not* going to be doing a science project for Wayne," Patti said firmly. "Because we're going to win!" I glanced at her. She *was* serious all right!

"Win what?" Stephanie asked. "The dogsled race?" She giggled. "Bullwinkle would end up dragging us to Dannerville." Dannerville is about ten miles in the opposite direction from Munn's Pond, where the race was supposed to end. "Hey, Patti, I've got an idea. Maybe you could program Oddjob to pull us."

"I don't think robots are allowed in a dogsled race," Kate said seriously.

"Unless they're robot *dogs*," I added.

"Odd-dog!" Stephanie said. That cracked us both up.

We reached the glass doors at the front of the mall. They slid silently open. A blast of cold air made our eyes water. I could see Roger's headlights shining across the parking lot.

"He's got the motor running," Kate warned, picking up speed.

It's hard to race across a sheet of icy snow while you're carrying a big pizza box. But I made it into the backseat of the car just as Roger shifted into first gear.

"Cutting it pretty close, Lauren," he grumbled. "Another second and you would have been walking home." He smiled at me in the rearview mirror. Roger can be really grouchy, but all in all I have to admit he's not so bad. Since Stephanie's mom had been expecting a baby, I'd thought a lot about what I'd prefer in a sibling, if I could have my choice. I'd rather have a brother than a sister. But I think that's just because Roger seems so great next to Kate's sister, Melissa-the-Monster. Of course, if Roger were a younger brother, filling the house with bugs and lizards — like Horace, who loves creepy-crawlies — I might feel differently.

The car radio was tuned to WBRM, the Riverhurst rock and roll station. Roger had it turned up pretty loud, so we couldn't really talk about the Winter Carnival. We probably wouldn't have talked about it anyway, not in front of Roger. He doesn't usually think much of our schemes.

He drove us to our house, and dropped us off at the back door. We dashed into the kitchen and struggled out of our coats, scarves, and hats.

We piled trays with the pizza, two bottles of Dr Pepper, and a king-size bag of sour-cream-and-onion potato chips. Then we carried the food upstairs to my room along with the box of chocolates from Sweet Stuff for dessert.

When my bedroom door was firmly closed behind us, I turned to Patti and said, "You didn't really mean it about dogsledding, did you?"

Patti blushed, stared at her wet sneakers, and said, "I can't back down now, Lauren. Not after what

23

Wayne Miller said about the Quarks. I'm really getting tired of being called a weirdo or an egghead because I like science. I just want to prove to Wayne Miller once and for all that there's nothing wimpy about people who like to study." Then she quietly added, "But this doesn't have to involve you guys. If Roger wouldn't mind lending me Bullwinkle, I think I can take care of it myself." Bullwinkle is officially Roger's dog, since Roger was the one who picked him out at the pound ten years ago.

"No way," Stephanie said. "We do everything together, don't we?" She grinned. "If *you're* going to take on Wayne Miller, we're *all* going to take on Wayne Miller!"

Kate and I both nodded. Then the four of us sat down on my rug, and everyone took a slice of pizza.

"The problem is, Bullwinkle is practically untrainable," I pointed out. "Once Mom and Dad spent two hundred dollars to enroll him at Canine Capers so that he'd learn to sit and stay and stuff like that. But Canine Capers didn't teach him a thing! The only command Bullwinkle really obeys is, 'Get your ball.' "

"Cats are supposed to be untrainable, and I managed to train Adelaide for the science fair," Patti reminded us. Adelaide is her black-and-white kitten, sister to Kate's Fredericka, Stephanie's Cinders, and my Rocky, who was sound asleep on my bottom bunk at that moment. "All I needed were some tasty snacks, and a lot of patience. . . ."

"We don't have time for patience," Kate said. "We've only got eight days. The race is next Saturday, and Wayne Miller said he's been practicing for weeks!"

"Kate's right." Patti said. "Maybe we ought to get started right away." Somehow I didn't think that was what Kate meant, but Patti's mind was racing ahead. She put down a half-eaten slice of pizza and leapt to her feet. "Where is Bullwinkle anyway, Lauren?"

"Locked up in the spare bedroom." We always keep Bullwinkle shut away during sleepovers. He gets awfully excited when we have company.

"Why don't we wait until Mom and Dad have gone to bed?" I suggested nervously. In my experience anything involving Bullwinkle has a way of turning into a complete disaster.

"Yeah," Kate agreed. I think she was still secretly hoping she'd be able to talk the rest of us out of it. Maybe she would have, too, if we hadn't decided to listen to WBRM.

WBRM is the only station we ever listen to. On Friday and Saturday nights, Rockin' Ralphie, our favorite deejay, takes special dedications over the phone. Mostly, it's high-school kids who call in, but we still like to guess who's who. That night we heard a request for "Love is Forever," from Todd S. to Mary Beth Y. That was an easy one. Todd Schwartz is the quarterback for the Riverhurst High football team and Mary Beth Young is his girlfriend. Everyone knows who they are because they seem to spend their lives breaking up and getting back together again.

"I guess the fighting's over for this week," Stephanie said knowingly. She took another bite of her pizza.

More dedications poured in. We polished off the pizza and potato chips, and started on the candy. And then we heard *it*.

"From Wayne M. to those four girls in 5B. Wayne says, you know who you are!" Rockin' Ralphie announced for all of Riverhurst to hear.

"He means us!" Stephanie exclaimed, thunderstruck.

"By those heavy-metal heavyweights, the Fat Guys," Rockin' Ralphie went on, "here comes, 'Losers!' "

"We'll see about that!" Kate growled. She scrambled to her feet and pulled open the door to my bedroom.

"Where are you going?" I asked her. Kate looked so mad I thought she might be planning to march straight over to Wayne's house and give him a piece of her mind.

"I'm going to use the phone!" she said in a slightly lower voice, since my parents' bedroom is just a few feet away.

Kate stepped into the hall, grabbed the hall phone, and pulled it back into my room.

"Six, seven, three, four, eight, nine, five. Call in with those dedications!" said Rockin' Ralphie. "Call now. The lines are free and Rockin' Ralphie's waiting."

Kate frowned and punched the buttons. "Hello," Kate said after a moment. "WBRM? . . . I'd like to make a request. . . . Yes, that's right. To Wayne M. in 5A from those four girls in 5B: 'Fools Can Never Win' by the Dominoes. You've got it . . . Thank you."

Kate hung up the phone. We waited for a few minutes. Then the request came on. Kate listened with a satisfied smile. Then she carried the phone back into the hall. "The lights are out in your parents' room, Lauren," she said when she came back. "They must be asleep! Let's get to work."

I turned off my radio, and the four of us crept out of my bedroom and down the hall.

The spare room is right at the top of the stairs. Before I even touched the knob, I could hear Bullwinkle on the other side of the door whining and scratching. My parents might have been asleep, but Bullwinkle was ready and waiting!

"Brace yourselves," I whispered. Slowly, I turned the doorknob, hoping he'd stay calm.

But as soon as Bullwinkle heard the click of the lock, he threw all of his weight against the door, and hurtled into the hall!

"Oh, no! He'll wake up my parents!" I whispered as Bullwinkle raced toward their bedroom. Now that my parents are both working, they're tired at night. I knew they wouldn't appreciate Bullwinkle's idea of a friendly hello — which is jumping on top of you, whether you're asleep or not!

"Grab him!" Kate hissed.

When Roger picked him out at the pound ten years ago he was a little black puppy. Everyone said he was mostly cocker spaniel. But he turned out to be mostly *Newfoundland.* Not only does he weigh 130 pounds, but he's over five feet tall when he stands up on his hind legs!

Grabbing Bullwinkle is no small chore.

But I managed to wrap my arms around his neck. Then I dug in my heels like a steer wrestler in a rodeo. Bullwinkle was still lumbering forward, dragging me along with him. But then Patti lunged for one of his front legs; Stephanie lunged for the other, and Kate grabbed his thick, furry tail. We finally managed to stop him, only a few feet away from my parents' door.

"Turn him around," Stephanie whispered in my ear.

"How?" I whispered back. Then I had an idea. "Candy," I said. "We've got to get some candy!"

Stephanie nodded and let go of one of Bullwinkle's legs. Bullwinkle seemed to have sort of forgotten where he wanted to go. Instead of lurching forward, he only licked my head in a casual but friendly way.

Stephanie was back in a flash with a big chunk of chocolate bark and bag of dog treats.

"Just a little candy," I warned. "Otherwise, he'll get wild ideas!"

Stephanie nodded and broke off a small piece. She waved it under Bullwinkle's nose. It certainly got his attention! One bite, and Bullwinkle was ready to follow Stephanie anywhere. In fact, when she tiptoed toward the stairs, he swung around in such a hurry Kate, Patti, and I almost went crashing into the wall.

It was kind of tricky for a while, keeping Bullwinkle from running *over* Stephanie. But once we'd gotten him down to the kitchen and closed the doors, we were home free.

Chapter
4

"Safe!" Kate panted.

"Easy for you to say," said Stephanie. She'd had to jump onto a chair to keep the chocolate and dog treats out of the reach of Bullwinkle's teeth. "Now what?"

"Does he have a harness?" Patti asked me.

I nodded. "He has one from his obedience classes at Canine Capers," I said. "I'll get it."

The harness was bright red. It had been stuffed into the back of our hall closet. I looked it over. It was kind of wrinkled, but otherwise it was okay. I found two leashes, too, and carried them all to the kitchen.

Bullwinkle *is* definitely a little frisky, but he's

basically a really nice dog. He let Kate and me strap the harness on him with no complaints. Meanwhile, Patti and Stephanie fed him the dog treats.

"There! Doesn't he look spiffy?" Kate said when we'd finished.

Bullwinkle *did* look nice with the red harness gleaming against his glossy black fur.

"If appearance counts, he'll win, hands down," Stephanie agreed from the chair. "Killer Miller is about the scraggliest looking dog I've ever seen."

"We'll need something to attach the harness to the sled," Patti said, studying Bullwinkle carefully.

"What about these?" I suggested, holding up the leashes.

"Great!" Patti nodded. "All we have to do is fasten the snaps to either side of the harness."

While she bent down to do just that, Stephanie slipped Bullwinkle another treat to keep him occupied. Patti straightened up, with a pleased expression on her face. "We can tie the other ends to the front of the sled. Now all we need is the sled."

"We're not actually going to try this right now, are we?" Stephanie protested. "It's midnight, and it's freezing outside! It's also snowing again!" She pointed dramatically out the kitchen window, where snowflakes were swirling down thick and fast. "I don't know about you guys, but I don't particularly want to catch pneumonia."

"So we'll do it in the kitchen instead," I said, "At least Bullwinkle can get the feel of it that way. If you all help me push the kitchen table and chairs against the wall, I'll slip on my coat and boots and run out to the garage for the sled."

We had an old wooden sled in the garage that belonged to my dad when he was a kid. It's really neat. It curves up on the sides to hold you in and has little red reindeer painted on it. Roger used the sled when he was small. Then I did. We may occasionally lose things in my family, but we *never* throw anything away.

By the time I'd dragged the sled out of the garage and up the back steps to the kitchen, Kate and Patti had moved the kitchen table and all the chairs (except the one Stephanie was still perched on) into the hall. Bullwinkle was still sitting in exactly the same position. His big, shiny black eyes were fixed on the dog treats in Stephanie's hand.

Patti tied the loose ends of the leashes to the front of the sled with a couple of anchor knots. "We're all set," she said cheerfully. I couldn't believe how seriously Patti was taking this. "The lightest of us should sit in the sled. . . ."

"That would be Kate," Stephanie said quickly.

"Fine with me." Kate plopped down on the sled. "It'll be my pleasure to run Wayne Miller into the ground. Or into the snow, I'm not particular."

"I never thought I'd see the day when I'd be glad to say I'm heavier than somebody else," Stephanie murmured. Stephanie's always complaining about her weight, although she isn't fat at all.

Kate giggled. "Giddyap, Bullwinkle, or whatever it is you say to sled dogs."

"You say *Mush!*" I told her. "Don't you remember *Admiral Peary: Discoverer of the North Pole?*" That's a movie Kate and I have seen at least five times, maybe more.

"Oh, yeah, you're right. Mush!" Kate commanded Bullwinkle, sternly.

He didn't even bother to turn his head.

"Mush! Mush!" Stephanie and I shouted. There was no response.

"We're not getting very far with this," Kate commented, lounging back in the sled.

"Bullwinkle just needs a little encouragement," Patti said earnestly. "I read a book about huskies once. It said that the new dogs were trained by putting them in harness with old dogs, until they got the idea. And since we don't have an experienced dog. . . ." She took a dog treat from Stephanie and held it out in front of Bullwinkle. Then, before he could snatch it out of her hand, Patti started moving backward as fast as she could.

Bullwinkle bounded after her. When he hit the ends of his leashes, Kate and the sled took a giant leap across the kitchen floor!

It must have been a pretty bumpy ride. Luckily, Kate managed to grab the sides of the sled and hang on. "Whoa!" she squeaked. "Whoa, Bullwinkle, stop!"

Bullwinkle came to a halt and looked around to see why Kate was making such a fuss. He cocked his head, puzzled.

Patti hurriedly fed him another treat. "Sorry, Kate, I'll try to make it smoother next time," she said. "Come on, Bullwinkle. Look at me!"

After that Patti walked slowly but steadily in a big circle around the kitchen. Bullwinkle followed her, dragging the sled with Kate on it behind him. He looked as though he'd been doing it all his life!

"I think it's working," I said.

"It's actually kind of fun!" Kate grinned.

"I'll bet. But one of us can't run in front of Bullwinkle for the whole race, slipping him dog treats," Stephanie pointed out. "It's not good for him, for one thing. But if we don't" — she raised her eyebrows — "who knows what will happen?"

Just then Patti gave Bullwinkle the last treat. As soon as he saw there wasn't anymore coming Bullwinkle sat down and refused to budge.

"You see what I mean?" Stephanie said. "When the treats are gone, Bullwinkle becomes instantly untrainable."

"We can't run along with him," Patti said. "But how about if we dangled some food in front of him? Sort of like the old donkey-with-the-carrot-on-a-stick trick?"

Patti isn't known as a brain for nothing. "Great idea! There are some more dog treats in the kitchen, and Bullwinkle likes them better than anything else. We could hang them off the end of my dad's fishing pole," I said. "That way, Kate can raise or lower it if she wants to."

"Let's give it a try," Patti said. "You go get the dog treats and we'll see if it works."

"Maybe, we ought to try it outdoors, in the back-

36

yard," Kate suggested. She got out of the sled. "There's really not enough space in here to give Bullwinkle a fair test."

"Are you out of your mind?" Stephanie asked in a horrified voice. "Do you have any idea how cold it is out there? Besides, it's the middle of the night!"

"It's only eleven-something," I said. "Besides, if we're quiet, my parents will never know we went outside."

"But it's snowing even harder," Stephanie said.

"Hey, it is!" Patti said excitedly. "That's excellent! Bullwinkle needs to get in some practice in the snow, just in case there's a blizzard on the day of the race."

"Oh, brother." Stephanie snuggled deeper into her flannel nightgown. "You guys can go out there if you want. I'm staying put."

"We're all in this together, remember?" Kate reminded her. "You can't slide out of it now!"

"Oh, all right," Stephanie groaned.

We closed Bullwinkle up in the kitchen. Then we snuck upstairs to my bedroom and grabbed all the warm clothes we could find. We tiptoed downstairs carrying a big pile of coats, sweaters, scarves, and mittens, along with the box of dog treats from the kitchen.

Then I crept down to the basement and came back with my dad's fishing pole.

"How do you plan to attach the dog treat to that?" Stephanie asked, looking at the fish hook on the end. "I mean, Bullwinkle's not exactly a flounder."

"I know what to do," Patti said. First she cut the fish hook off the line. Then she made a hole in the middle of one of the bone-shaped dog treats with a nail. The fishing line went through the hole, and Patti tied it tight.

"You can hold the pole with one hand," she said, handing it to Kate, "and hold onto the sled with the other."

After that was settled, the four of us got dressed for the outdoor test. Stephanie must have been wearing about seven sweaters by the time she was finished.

"Let's try not to make any noise," I warned everybody. "My parents' window looks right into the backyard!"

I opened the back door, and we all tiptoed down the steps with Bullwinkle and the sled. Snow was falling as thick as confetti, covering the fence, the bird bath, and everything else in the backyard with a blanket of soft, white flakes.

"At least the wind has died down," Stephanie murmured. Her face was almost completely wrapped in a scarf.

She and Patti started feeding Bullwinkle dog treats. They had to to keep him from barking as loudly as he could or tearing around like a lunatic, the way he usually does when he goes outside.

Then we led Bullwinkle toward the back fence. I lined up the sled directly behind him, and looked out at the empty, snow-covered lawn. "There's nothing in his way," I said "Let's try him out."

Kate sat down on the sled and held the fishing pole so that the line dangled high over Bullwinkle's head.

"So far, so good," Patti whispered to Stephanie. "Now, step back. . . ."

Kate let out some of the fishing line, so that the dog treat dangled down about a foot in front of Bullwinkle's furry black nose.

He swiveled his head from side to side looking for Patti and Stephanie. He was trying to figure out what had happened to his delicious dog treat supply.

Then he raised his nose and sniffed the air. He'd picked up the scent. At last, he spotted the dog treat hanging on the fishing line! He leapt forward, trying to catch up with the tempting little bone-shaped biscuit. His nose wiggling eagerly, Bullwinkle trotted along faster and faster. The sled slid through the snow behind him with Kate hanging on for dear life.

"It's working!" Patti whispered gleefully.

"If you use your brain, you don't have to be like Wayne Miller and waste your time practicing for weeks!" I said. "Go! Bullwinkle, go!"

Chapter
5

Perhaps I shouldn't have cheered Bullwinkle on quite so enthusiastically.

Just then a big gust of wind came swirling through the backyard, blowing snow around, and making the dog treat swing back and forth. Bullwinkle lunged for it.

His lunge pushed the sled off balance. Kate fell forward and the fishing pole tipped further forward, bringing the dog treat even closer.

Bullwinkle snapped at it eagerly. He was determined to get that dog treat one way or another. Kate jerked the pole and dog treat back. Bullwinkle tried to follow it. Soon Bullwinkle, the sled, and Kate were moving around and around, in a tighter and tighter circle. It looked almost as if Bullwinkle were chasing his tail — only his tail was the sled with Kate still on it!

"I don't think this is how Admiral Peary did it," Stephanie murmured.

"Helllpp!" Kate wailed softly. "I'm getting seasick!" She was hanging onto the sled as tightly as she could with one hand. Her other hand was still glued to the fishing pole.

"Drop it!" Patti, Stephanie, and I said over and over again. "Drop the pole!"

I guess Kate was too panicked to do anything, because she hung onto the fishing pole as if her life depended on it.

Now, I can personally vouch for the fact that there's nothing wimpy about *some* kids with brains. While Stephanie and I were standing there paralyzed, Patti waded right into the middle of that tornado of dog, sled, and swirling snow. She grabbed Bullwinkle around his thick neck, and leaned into him with all of her weight. Now he was dragging not only the sled and Kate, but Patti, as well. It was too much even for Bullwinkle. Slowly but surely, he started to wind down.

We were all beginning to breathe sighs of relief

when suddenly the back door light came on and my dad hollered, "What on earth are you girls doing out there?" He was wearing his striped bathrobe, and he looked like he'd just woken up. "Don't you know it's the middle of the night, and there's a blizzard going on?"

He certainly made Stephanie and me jump — and our sled dog, too. Bullwinkle came to a sudden and complete halt. Kate flew up in the air and rolled out of the sled and into the snow. Patti ran to help her up.

It was a good thing Kate fell clear of the sled. As soon as Bullwinkle caught his breath and spotted Dad standing at the back door, he barked joyfully. Then he flung himself toward the house.

"No, Bullwinkle! *No!*" Dad thundered as he saw all 130 pounds of snow-covered animal come barreling toward him. "Sit! Bullwinkle. Stay!"

But "Sit!" and "Stay!" didn't seem to mean anything to Bullwinkle. He raced toward the back steps, and clambered up them as fast as he could, paying absolutely no attention to the sled, which he was still pulling behind him.

The sled's runners hooked under the bottom step, and the sled began to splinter, and so did the step. Part of Bullwinkle's harness ripped off, but that didn't worry him. He just kept going until he was where he wanted to be. Standing up on his hind legs, he gave my father's face a long, wet lick.

"Down! Down!" my dad shouted. He looked sadly at the twisted wood and metal sled. "One of you better have a good explanation for all this," he said. "And you can start by telling me why the dog *smells* like dog treats!"

"That will have to wait, George." My mom came walking up to the kitchen door. "All of you get inside the house this minute, before you catch pneumonia." She peered down at us. "Stephanie, is that you under that pile of clothes?" she asked, herding us inside.

Stephanie nodded, peeling off scarves like the layers of an onion.

"Your father just called from the hospital. It looks as though your mother will be having the baby tonight!" Mom said.

"Wow!" Kate and Patti and I exclaimed.

Stephanie looked shocked. "What should I be doing?" she said. She sounded kind of worried.

"I don't think you'll have to do anything, sweetie," my mom said. "Your mom and her doctor will take care of that. And your dad will call as soon as he has some news. Why don't you girls go to bed? I'll wake you up as soon as I hear from him, I promise."

Stephanie shook her head. "I can't possibly *sleep*," she said.

"I thought that might be the case, so here's plan B," Mom told us. "You can all make hot chocolate and watch TV until Mr. Green calls back, okay? I'll even open a new box of cookies."

"That sounds terrific, Mrs. Hunter," Stephanie said gratefully.

My father was at the other end of the kitchen. He was busy swabbing off a dripping Bullwinkle with old bath towels. "Can somebody finish drying off this dog while I get the sled?" he asked.

"Sure." Kate and Patti took the towels and started rubbing down Bullwinkle's thick black fur. His silly face wore an expression of total contentment. As far as he was concerned, anyway, the sled driving lesson had been a complete success.

Dad stepped outside. A few seconds later, he reappeared carrying his sled. "Almost forty years old and barely a scratch," he announced sadly. "Now look at it!"

After one night with the Sleepover Friends —
and Bullwinkle — Dad's sled was a total wreck. Two
of the long boards on the front end were hanging
totally loose. One runner was bent completely out
of shape, and the cross-piece had torn off altogether.

My father sighed and shook his head.

"We're sorry, Dad," I said. I really meant it. My
father loves all his old stuff, like his sled, his ratty
old baseball glove, and a basketball he's had since
high school that's always going flat.

"We'll pay to have it fixed, Mr. Hunter," Kate
said.

"Or maybe we can win a new one for you!"
Patti said. We all looked at her. Wasn't she willing
to give up yet?

"Win a sled? How would you do that?" my father asked her.

So we told him about the contests at the Winter
Carnival and about our fight with Wayne Miller.

"If I were that boy, I wouldn't want to have you
girls mad at *me*," Dad said when we'd finished.
"Good luck, though. You'll need it, with Bullwinkle
as a sled dog. And, please — no more practicing
tonight, or Mrs. Green might have company at the
hospital."

46

"Yes, Mr. Hunter," Patti, Stephanie, and Kate said. My father wandered upstairs to bed. As soon as she'd put the cookies on the table, Mom followed him. Then Bullwinkle walked slowly into the living room, flopped down on the rug with a happy sigh, and fell fast asleep.

Kate stirred up some hot chocolate and dropped in a few marshmallows. Then we turned on the TV in the den.

"What do you guys want to watch?" I asked, picking up the remote. "Old movies? Reruns?" Friday is not the greatest night for TV in Riverhurst as far as I'm concerned.

"We ought to be able to catch part of Friday Chillers," Stephanie said, still looking completely distracted.

Usually I would have argued, since scary movies really don't agree with me very well. But I thought it was important to take Stephanie's mind off things. She was looking a little agitated. So that's how we ended up watching the end of a very creepy movie called *The Terrible Twins*.

In the movie one sister locks her twin up in a tower. Then she takes her place and lives *her* life. She even marries the first twin's boyfriend. The twin locked up in the tower finally manages to escape, but by then she's totally bananas. "She could really use a make-over," was Stephanie's only comment.

After that, things went from bad to much, much worse. By the time the first twin showed up with an attack-trained chihuahua, I'd eaten at least a dozen cookies all by myself, out of sheer nervousness! I decided I couldn't take it anymore.

"That's enough," I said firmly and switched stations. Ignoring Kate's protests, I jumped past a horror movie on Channel 24 *and* a sci-fi rerun on 19 to Video Trax.

We all fell asleep listening to a Battle of the Bands live from Sydney, Australia. *I* didn't wake up until early the next morning. I was dreaming that Roger was my twin and he was trying to smother me with a hairy pillow for being late again. . . .

I blinked my eyes open. Bullwinkle was lying on the floor of the den near my head, his tail flopped over my face. Sunlight was streaming through the window.

The TV was still on, but the sound was turned way down. Kate and Stephanie were asleep on the couch, and Patti was lying flopped out across our old brown armchair. "Stephanie — Stephanie!" I said. "Wake up! Maybe you're a sister!"

"As long as I'm not a twin," she mumbled drowsily.

Then she sat up and rubbed her eyes. "Oh, no!" she said. "I must have fallen asleep. I better call my father!"

But my mom stuck her head around the door from the kitchen. "Calm down, Stephanie. Your dad called back last night, to say it was a false alarm. He and your mother went home again. All of you were sleeping so soundly that I didn't bother to wake you."

So Stephanie was still an only child, at least for a few more days.

Chapter
6

Later that morning, over a breakfast of banana waffles with blueberry syrup, Kate, Patti, Stephanie, and I had a serious talk about the carnival.

"I'm afraid I just don't think it's going to work with Bullwinkle," I told them.

Stephanie sighed. "Maybe we should forget the whole thing," she said in a discouraged voice. "You could have gotten creamed last night, Kate, just like the sled."

"Well, I'm not anxious to try it again," Kate agreed.

"I guess that means I'll have to do Wayne's next science project," Patti said slowly. I could tell she was upset even though she was trying not to show it.

"I don't see why," Stephanie said. "We'll just pretend it never really happened."

"I can't back down," Patti objected. "We shook on it!"

"Who's going to believe Wayne Miller, or Ronny Wallace either, for that matter?" Stephanie said.

"That's not the point," Patti said. "It's the principle of the thing." That was a phrase my father used a lot. But Patti was right. She'd shaken hands and it would be rotten to try to wriggle out of it.

Just then Bullwinkle, who was in the backyard, started barking his head off.

"He'll bark at anything," I said, spearing another waffle. "From a snowflake to a sparrow." I was losing patience with Bullwinkle.

But he wouldn't stop. Finally, I got up from the table and looked out the back door.

Bullwinkle was standing up on his hind legs, his front paws resting on the top of our fence. His head was turned toward the front of the house, and he was barking and growling like there was no tomorrow.

"He must see *something*. . . ," I said.

I walked into the living room and peered out one of the front windows. When I saw what Bullwinkle was barking at, I almost began to growl myself.

"Come quick!" I called to Kate, Stephanie, and Patti. "It's Wayne and Killer Miller!"

"You're kidding!" They jumped out of their chairs and raced into the living room just in time to see Killer pulling Wayne Miller and his sled down Pine Street.

Killer is a big, raw-boned, dirty-brown dog. He always has one ear up and one ear down, and his thin tail curls over his back.

"He sure is ugly," Kate said, staring at Killer.

"He looks exactly like a hyena!" I agreed.

"Who? Killer or Wayne?" Stephanie began to giggle.

"Never mind that," Kate said glumly. "I hate to admit it, but that dog knows how to pull a sled."

Kate was right. Wayne and Killer were *mushing* along like Admiral Peary and his team on their way to the North Pole. Killer was wearing a dark-green harness, hooked with these really professional-looking straps to a long wooden sled.

"What a show-off." Stephanie said. "He came here just to rub our noses in it. Watch out!" She pulled us away from the window as Wayne glanced toward my house. "Don't give him the satisfaction of knowing we've seen him."

"The depressing truth is, we *have* seen him!" said Kate with a frown. She flopped down on the living room couch. "I'm afraid Bullwinkle doesn't stand a chance!"

"What are we going to do?" I said, dropping onto the couch next to her. "It makes me absolutely *sick* to think that Wayne Miller is better at *anything* than we are."

"Me, too," Stephanie agreed. "We can't give up without a fight!"

"I'll bet Bullwinkle is as fast as Killer, and I'm sure he's a lot stronger," Patti said thoughtfully. "If I could just come up with a way to direct his energy. . . ."

"I think we'd better diversify," Stephanie said. She stood up and closed the curtains, shutting Wayne out.

"Where did you get that word?" I asked her. "From your dad?" Stephanie picks up a lot of lawyer talk from her father. She's always using expressions

53

like, "I rest my case," and "Objection overruled."

"Nope — from Nana," Stephanie said. "It means to try lots of different things."

"What exactly did you have in mind?" Kate asked her.

"The snow sculpture contest?" I suggested. "If Wayne and Ronny can do it, so can we."

"I might even consider trying out for snow maiden," Stephanie announced.

"You would?" Patti said with a shiver. "Get up on a stage in front of all those people?"

"Why not?" Stephanie shrugged. "It's one contest Wayne Miller *can't* possibly win. . . ."

"But you'll need a talent," Kate said. "A third of the score is for appearance, and the rest is for talent. I heard some of the sixth-graders talking about it at lunch this week."

"No problem. I'll sing," Stephanie said.

Kate raised an eyebrow at Patti and me. Stephanie does *not* have as good a voice as she thinks she does.

"Or maybe you could dance," I suggested hurriedly.

"Or something," Kate murmured. "We also

have to come up with a design for our snow sculpture," she went on. "We'll need to practice it before next weekend."

"I have a dentist's appointment this afternoon," Patti said. "But why don't you guys come over to my house tomorrow? We can use my mom's gardening tools to help us make our sculpture."

"Fine," Kate said. "That'll give us some time to get ideas."

"Wayne Miller's going to be very sorry he ever decided to cross us," I said. I hoped I sounded more positive than I felt. Who would have thought Wayne Miller would be so hard to beat?

That afternoon I had to go grocery shopping with my mom. But after dinner I flipped through a stack of old magazines in our basement looking for possible sculpture subjects. I knew if I didn't go to Patti's the next day with at least a couple of good ideas, Kate would jump all over me.

Stephanie was already at Patti's house when Dr. Beekman dropped Kate and me off on Sunday. We could hear them laughing as we rang the front door-

55

bell. We didn't hear anything for a second. Then the door swung open.

"Oddjob!" Kate exclaimed. The small silver robot rolled backwards. His metal fingers pulled the door open even wider.

"Please . . . come . . . in," Oddjob said in his crackly voice. "Follow . . . me."

The robot led us down the hall to the Jenkinses' kitchen.

"Isn't he neat?" Stephanie said. She and Patti were sitting at the kitchen table, having Cokes and cheese doodles. "Wait till you see what else Patti's programmed him to do!"

"Actually, Horace helped me," Patti said. "I couldn't have done it alone. Oddjob — drinks, please."

The robot whirred and clicked for a second, digesting Patti's order. Then he swung around, and opened the refrigerator door. He grabbed a bottle of Coke with one metal hand, and unscrewed the cap with the other.

Then Oddjob rolled over to the counter. Lifting his arm, he poured the Coke into two glasses that were sitting next to the sink. He picked up a glass in each hand and came back to the table. With a whir and a click, he set the full glasses down in front of us.

"Two . . . drinks," Oddjob announced.

Kate and I both clapped.

"Thanks," Patti said. "By Friday, maybe I'll have him making Alaska dip!" Our sleepover the following Friday was going to be at Patti's house. Alaska dip is one of her special recipes.

"We'll have plenty to do this week without messing around with Oddjob," Kate said in a tone that said she meant business. "Does anyone have suggestions for our snow sculpture?"

"What about a castle?" I said. "I saw a picture in an old magazine of a fabulous one in China. They made the whole thing out of snow and ice, with towers and turrets and everything. You could actually walk inside it."

"That sounds beautiful, Lauren," Patti said.

Kate shook her head. "Too complicated," she said. "I'll bet there were hundreds of Chinese working on it, and there are only four of us."

"What about a snow rabbit or a polar bear?"

Stephanie suggested. "It's basically like making a snowman, but a little more interesting."

"Or a group of penguins," Patti said, her face lighting up. "I have something to show you in one of our natural history books. . . ."

She raced out of the kitchen into the living room. Like practically every other room in the Jenkinses' house, it has floor-to-ceiling bookshelves against two walls. Patti's parents are professors at the university in Riverhurst and they read all the time. Patti and Horace both read all the time, too. That means a lot of books.

Patti came back carrying a large, heavy book called, *Animals and Birds of the Northern Hemisphere*, Volume 2. She flipped to a page titled "Penguins." Then she held up a photograph for all of us to see. It showed a group of four of them standing in a circle with their heads together.

Stephanie giggled. "They look almost like they're gossiping."

Patti nodded. "I think I like the picture so much because they reminded me of us. Notice how two are shorter, and two are taller? The tall ones can be Lauren and me."

"They're great!" I said. "I especially like the way they're holding out their wings, or flippers, or whatever they're called. It looks like they're about to hug each other. They're so cute!"

Kate liked the penguins, too. For one thing they were practical. "We'd need three round balls to make each of them," she said, narrowing her eyes. "And a little beak cut out of paper, and for eyes we could. . . ." She started pulling on her coat, even though she'd just taken it off. "Come on, you guys. Let's go outside and try it."

Patti borrowed some of her mom's gardening tools from the shed in the backyard. She collected shovels, trowels, and anything else that looked like it would help us scoop snow up or pack it down.

In a couple of hours, we had completely lined the Jenkinses' patio with penguins. There were short ones, tall ones, fat ones, and thin ones. They all had funny little paper beaks and dark stones for eyes.

"We need more practice, of course," Kate said, standing back to look over the whole group. "But I like them. We're definitely on the right track."

"Maybe we should add black jackets and red bowties," Stephanie suggested.

I know red and black are Stephanie's favorite colors, but what else can you do with penguins? "Good idea," I said.

"We'll try it next time," said Patti, opening the back door. We all trooped after her. After two hours of digging around in the snow, we were all more than ready to sit around Patti's warm kitchen!

As soon as we stepped inside, we could hear Oddjob's high tinny voice. "My turn," he was saying. "Bishop to knight five!"

"Horace!" Patti yelped.

We hurried into the kitchen to find Patti's little brother sitting at the table with Oddjob. A chessboard was between them.

"Horace, Oddjob does not play chess!" Patti said sternly.

"He does now," Horace replied with an absorbed look on his face. "Sssh!" He put his finger to his lips. "We're concentrating."

"Mom! Dad!" Patti yelled as Oddjob reached out to move his bishop.

"You're just jealous because you didn't think of it first, Patti!" Horace muttered with a scowl.

"Horace, that's not true," Patti began. But he just put his hands over his ears.

"I hear my dad's car outside," Kate said quickly. "Come on, Lauren and Stephanie. Patti, we'll see you tomorrow."

We retreated down the front hall and out the front door before the argument really got going.

"Horace used to be such a nice little boy," Stephanie said as the three of them headed for Dr. Beekman's red Volkswagen.

"Well, he's not so bad even now," Kate said with a sigh. "Just look at Melissa!"

Melissa was sitting in the front seat next to Kate's dad. When she saw us coming, she stuck her tongue out at us, and pressed her whole face flat against the window.

"Ick!" said Stephanie. "I used to think I'd rather have a sister. At least we'd be interested in the same things. . . ."

"Fat chance," Kate put in gloomily.

"Then I decided a brother might be easier," Stephanie said, stopping next to the car. "Because of Horace. But look at what's happening to him!"

"They all get older," Kate reminded her.

"Yeah, but do they all get worse?" Stephanie wondered aloud.

"Roger's okay," I said. I tried to sound encouraging.

"But by the time your brother or sister is Roger's age, you'll be twenty-eight, and none of it will matter."

"Thanks, Kate," Stephanie said with a sigh. "I'll hold on to that thought." Then we climbed into the backseat of Dr. Beekman's car.

Chapter
7

The week seemed to pass by in a flash. We had something to do every minute of the day. There was school, of course, and after school we had to practice our snow sculptures. Then there was Stephanie's routine to work on for the Snow Maiden contest. We'd convinced her to lip-synch "Get Down," by the Bounder Sisters, while doing a dance number. Stephanie may not have the best voice in the world, but she's a great dancer.

We even patched Bullwinkle's torn halter, just in case Patti could think of a way to handle him in the dogsled race. As I said, we were busy all the time. And before we knew it, it was Friday afternoon.

The final bell had rung at Riverhurst Elementary.

The four of us were standing outside the school waiting for Mrs. Jenkins to pick us up and drive us to the carnival. All of a sudden, we spotted Wayne Miller standing with Mark Freedman, Kyle Hubbard, and some of the other fifth-grade guys a few feet away.

"Four girls, and one of them a Quack, or whatever those geeks are called," he was saying. "Get real. Of course I'm going to beat 'em!"

"I wouldn't be so sure, Wayne," Kyle Hubbard said. "I know Kate, and Kate doesn't give up. Neither do the rest of them." Kyle and Kate got to be friends last year, when they were in the same fourth-grade class.

"Yeah, I'd watch it, Wayne," Mark Freedman said. "As a matter of fact, I'm willing to bet you my New York Mets caps that Kate, Lauren, Stephanie, and Patti will blow you away in the dog-sled race." I couldn't believe my ears. Mark is a baseball nut, and some Mets players had actually signed his cap. It was his favorite possession.

"Oh, no!" Patti whispered. "Mark loves that cap! We can't let him lose it."

Wayne eyed Mark with a greedy grin on his face. "I could use a new cap," he said. "Why not take yours?"

64

"Hold on a second. What'll you give me if you lose?" Mark asked him.

"No way I can lose," Wayne said. "But on the off chance that Killer gets a sprained ankle or something . . . I guess I'd give you my baseball, autographed by Billy Peyton."

"Who's Billy Peyton?" Stephanie whispered.

"A catcher for the Los Angeles Dodgers," I answered.

"There's Mom," Patti said.

As Mrs. Jenkins pulled up to the curb and we opened the car doors, the guys spotted us.

"Hey, Kate — Lauren — good luck on Sunday!" Kyle yelled.

"Yeah. Extra-good luck. I'm counting on you," Mark Freedman added, pointing to the blue cap he was wearing.

"What are we going to do now?" Stephanie said, scooting into the backseat of Mrs. Jenkins's car. "We can't let Wayne get away with this!"

"I'm thinking, I'm thinking," Patti mumbled. "There's something somebody said about Bullwinkle. . . . but, I just can't seem to remember it."

Patti's mom drove Kate, Stephanie, and me to our houses to pick up our overnight stuff. We all got out at Stephanie's house, to say hello to Mrs. Green. She hadn't had the baby yet, but it was due any day. Nana, Stephanie's grandmother, was spending the weekend. After we visited for a while, we went to Riverside Park, which is where the Winter Carnival is held.

The Riverhurst Carnival Committee had strung hundreds of strings of tiny white lights in the pine trees along the banks of the Pequontic — *the* river in "Riverhurst." They'd set up lots of booths, too, built to look like old-fashioned cottages. It was twilight. Lanterns were glowing in the booths, shining across the snow and onto the icy river.

"It looks so pretty!" Mrs. Jenkins exclaimed. "Like a village in northern Europe." Mrs. Jenkins is a history professor, and northern Europe is her specialty.

"It smells pretty nice, too," I said, sniffing the air like Bullwinkle does. People in the booths were selling hot apple cider, doughnuts, grilled sausages, candied apples, and lots of other good things to eat. Two women were making hand-dipped candles and evergreen wreaths. There was even a blacksmith hammering out iron forks and spoons next to a blazing hot fire.

"The dogsled race starts just past the last booth," Kate said. "I remember it from last year. The finish line's about a half a mile away, where the Pequontic widens into Munn's Pond."

"And there's the stage for the Snow Maiden contest," Stephanie cried.

The stage was set back in a circle of snow-covered pines, and raised about six feet off the ground. It looked really beautiful. "My red-and-black parka's going to look great against the snow and the trees," Stephanie said. "I just hope I don't freeze to death standing up there."

"The weather is supposed to be warmer tomorrow," Mrs. Jenkins said encouragingly. "I heard it on my car radio on the way to pick you up."

"It can't get too warm for me," Stephanie said shivering. "I'm just not a winter person. Come on. Let's get some of that hot apple cider down our throats."

We drank cider and ate sausages on rolls, and freshly made doughnuts. We even bought some candles at the candle-makers' booth. They smelled of pine and elderberry. Then, at last, we drove back to Patti's house.

As soon as we'd stepped into the kitchen, Patti

opened the door to her father's study. "Mom," she cried. "Where's Oddjob? He's not in here!"

"Horace!" Mrs. Jenkins called out.

"Yeah, Mom," Horace called back. The living room door opened, and rock music came blasting out. "What's up? Oddjob and I are watching Video Trax together."

"Are you sure that's *all* you're doing with Oddjob?" Mrs. Jenkins asked him.

"Of course, Mom," Horace said with a sly, lopsided grin. "Dad said it was okay."

Patti looked at us and raised her eyebrows.

"Who knows what he'll have Oddjob doing next?" she whispered.

"Well, turn off that noise and wash your hands," Mrs. Jenkins said. "We're going to have dinner soon."

As sleepovers go, the one at Patti's that night was strictly business. Stephanie did her routine for us again and again. Finally even Patti and I could have done all the steps in our sleep and we aren't what you'd call serious dancers.

Afterward all four of us bundled up again, turned on the Jenkinses' outdoor lights, and went outside. Then we got busy. We scooped up snow and packed it down until we'd added six more penguins to the seven that were already there. They looked pretty funny all lined up along the Jenkinses' patio.

"Can we please stop?" Stephanie said at last. "My lips are totally blue. So are my fingers, and blue isn't exactly my favorite color!"

"Yeah, can we?" I said. "By now I could make a snow penguin blindfolded."

"All right," Patti finally agreed. "At least we won't have the Snow Maiden and sculpture contests to worry about. We've given them our best shot."

Kate nodded. "Wayne *can't* beat us in the first one," she said. "And what judge wouldn't pick a nice bunch of penguins over Rambo-in-the-snow?"

But we'd forgotten about the weather.

Patti woke us up the next morning. "Red alert, red alert, guys!" she said. I opened my eyes reluctantly. It was barely light outside.

"What's the matter?" I asked sleepily. Patti and I were sharing the double bed.

Kate and Stephanie both groaned from sleeping bags on the floor, and turned over.

"Don't you hear that?" Patti said to me.

I listened and closed my eyes again. "Yeah, I

hear Adelaide snoring," I said. Patti's kitten was curled up on the pillow on the desk chair.

"No — the dripping!" Patti said. "Remember Mom told us it was supposed to get warmer? Well, it has — a *lot* warmer! The snow is all melting!"

"Warm is good," Stephanie mumbled from the floor.

"Not for snow sculptures," Patti said darkly.

"Oh, no!" I threw the covers back and scrambled out of bed. I stared through the window down at the patio below. Our sculptures no longer looked like a crowd of friendly penguins. Instead, they'd turned into a jumble of oddly shaped little lumps!

"Now what?" Kate said. She joined Patti and me at the window. Then she shook her head. "It doesn't look good," she said.

"Lauren, didn't you say the castle you saw in a magazine was made of snow and *ice*?" Patti asked me.

"That's right," I said. "Big blocks of ice."

"I think that would solve our problem," Patti cried. "Ice doesn't melt as quickly as snow. Bring the picture, Lauren. We'll make an ice castle instead!"

"But how are we going to get enough ice?" Kate

asked. "*One* block costs two dollars at Speedy Shop!"

"There's plenty of ice on the Pequontic. The water's frozen solid near the banks," Patti said. "And I think Oddjob can help us with it."

"How?" Stephanie was finally awake.

"He already saws wood," Patti said. "With a little fixing, I think I can make him saw ice, too."

Kate's eyes met mine and we both smiled quickly.

We'd learned one thing in the last week anyway. When Patti Jenkins decides to do something, there's no stopping her!

Chapter
8

After a breakfast of blueberry pancakes with real maple syrup, Kate, Stephanie, and I went home to change our clothes for the carnival. We'd all agreed to meet at ten-fifteen at the blacksmith's booth. The Snow Maiden contest would begin at ten-thirty.

At ten after ten, my dad dropped off Kate and me.

"I'll bet Stephanie has been here for an hour already, and she's gone over her routine as least four or five times," Kate grumbled as we hurried past the cider and sausage booths.

But when we reached the blacksmith's booth Stephanie was nowhere to be seen. Patti and Oddjob were there, though, and Patti grinned when she saw us.

"Did you fix him?" I asked Patti, pointing at Oddjob.

"I hope so," Patti said. "Dad is borrowing an ice-saw from a friend of his in the biology department. He'll bring it to us at twelve. Do you have the picture of the castle?"

The three of us were studying it when Mr. Morgan, the Mayor of Riverhurst, climbed onto the stage. He tapped the microphone. "Testing, testing," he said.

Kate looked at her watch. "It is ten-twenty. Stephanie better hurry up."

"I have an announcement to make," Mayor Morgan said. "One of our contestants, Miss Stephanie Green, will not be appearing, because her mother has gone to the hospital."

"Mrs. Green is having the baby!" I said.

"Did she have to have it now?" Kate groaned.

Patti didn't say anything.

Suddenly, we heard someone yell, "Quitters, quitters!" We looked around. Wayne and Ronny were standing near the stage, hooting and hollering in our direction. Wayne was singing the chorus of "Losers" just loud enough for us to hear.

Before we could shout back, though, Todd Schwartz came bounding up to us. As soon as they saw him, Wayne and Ronny got really quiet.

Besides being the high-school quarterback, Todd happens to live across the street from Stephanie on Pine.

"Hi, kids," he said to us. "Stephanie told me I'd find you here. She ran into me on her way to the hospital this morning. She asked me to give you her cassette player and tape. She said Lauren or Patti would know what to do with them." Todd handed the cassette player to Patti. "See ya," he said. Then he waved and trotted off to the candle-maker's booth, where he'd left his on-again, off-again girlfriend, Mary Beth Young.

"Great," I said, turning my back on Wayne and Ronny, who were starting up their hollering again. "What *are* we supposed to do with them?"

Patti coughed. "Take Stephanie's place," she said.

"No way. Not me," I said. I have such terrible stage fright that I don't even like to *talk* about it. Even thinking about going up there was making my knees knock together.

Patti sighed. "If you won't then I guess I'll have to. . . ."

"Get up on stage and dance?" said Kate. "Patti Jenkins, have you gone out of your mind?"

"Well, I'm not exactly dressed for it," Patti said, looking down at her green down parka and her fake-fur snow boots. "But I can't let Wayne Miller get away with calling me a Quack *and* a quitter!"

The contestants had started to line up across the back of the stage. There were a bunch of sixth-graders and Christy Soames from 5C and Tracy Osner from 5A. Patti clutched Stephanie's cassette recorder and marched bravely up the ramp and joined the line.

"How do we get Oddjob to move?" Kate asked, nudging the robot.

"I have no idea," I said.

So Kate and I stayed where we were, next to the blacksmith's booth, with the small silver man between us.

Mayor Morgan said a few words, and introduced the judges. They were Mrs. Milton, one of the teachers at our elementary school; Mr. Warren, the Fire

Chief; and Mrs. Petitt, the owner of Just Juniors, our favorite kids' store at the mall.

The contest began. First came a sixth-grade baton twirler. Then Christy Soames stood up and sang a slow, soppy song. . . .

"Awful!" Kate muttered. "And I'm even wearing earmuffs!"

Another sixth-grader did a tap dance, and then it was Patti's turn.

"Now give a big hand for. . . ," Mayor Morgan looked at her. Patti told him her name so softly, he had to lean forward to hear her. " . . . Patti Jenkins."

Wayne and Ronny had moved closer to the stage, but Patti was concentrating too hard to notice them. She put the cassette player down on an empty chair and switched it on.

We heard the thump-thumpety-thump of the drums at the beginning of "Get Down." Patti was waiting until the Bounder Sisters sang the first "Get down . . ." to start the dance. Then, all of a sudden, Oddjob let out a stream of whirs and clicks!

"Who set him off?!" Kate whispered nervously, backing away from the robot.

"Get down!" the Bounder Sisters blared from the cassette player on the stage.

Suddenly Oddjob began to roll away from Kate and me on his metal treads! He was heading straight for Patti! We ran after him.

I guess Uncle Nick had programmed Oddjob not to run over anybody or anything because he managed to roll around all the booths and people. But even so the little robot had gathered quite a crowd by the time he'd reached the stage.

Oddjob rolled right up the ramp and over to Patti. She froze in the middle of Stephanie's dance and stared at Oddjob. She glanced over at us, her mouth open. Oddjob whirred and clicked some more. Then he started waving his Slinky arms in the air and swaying back and forth on his treads in time to the *thump* of "Get Down." Oddjob was dancing!

Patti started moving again. The two of them finished up "Get Down" like a couple on the Saturday-afternoon program "Dance Craze" on Channel 12. When Patti switched off the cassette, and the music stopped, Oddjob stopped, too.

Patti looked at Kate and me and mouthed "Horace!" Then she grinned.

Kate and I looked at each other. Horace must have programmed Oddjob to dance to rock and roll music. "It's a good thing, too!" Kate yelled to me over the tremendous burst of applause Patti and Odd-job were getting. "This is one contest we've almost definitely won!"

Then Kate nodded her head in the direction of Wayne Miller and Ronny Wallace. "And they don't look too happy about it either." she said. Kate was right. Wayne and Ronny looked mad enough to pop!

But in the end the tap dancer won first place and Patti won first runner-up. And the judges even made up a new category for her routine: Most Cre ative.

When the trophies were presented, Patti was given a silver one. It was a statue of a girl in a long, flowing dress with a crown on her head.

Patti grinned when she showed it to Kate and me. "I guess it's the Snow Maiden," she said. "But it should have been a little silver man instead, since it's really Oddjob's prize." Patti also won a twenty-five dollar gift certificate to any sponsor's store.

"All riiight," Kate said, when she saw it. "Only forty-five dollars to go on that jacket for the Greens' baby!"

We were feeling pretty great, but we didn't have time to stand around and gloat about our victory. It was almost twelve o'clock and time for the snow sculpture contest. We ran down to the riverbank.

Mr. Jenkins met us there with the ice-saw. The ice next to the bank was about a foot thick. As soon as Patti put the saw in his hand, Oddjob got right to work. He whirred, clicked, and sawed. In about thirty seconds a neat block of ice was sitting on the bank ready for us to use!

With Oddjob sawing, Patti and Mr. Jenkins carrying, and Kate and me stacking, the ice castle grew very quickly. Kate said later, it looked just like a larger version of a castle made of kids' wooden blocks. I thought it looked much better than that, but you get the idea.

The ice melted a little in the sun but that didn't bother us. In fact, it was a help, because it glued the ice-blocks together like cement.

Meanwhile, Wayne and Ronny were having lots of problems. The snow was too mushy for them to pack properly, so the walls of their fort kept leaning every which way. With every soggy handful the boys were getting wetter, and angrier. Finally, Wayne threw his shovel into the air in a total rage!

"Who cares about the dumb snow sculpture

contest?!'' he shouted loud enough for us to hear. "It's for sissies, anyway."

We saw him say something to Ronny, and then a chorus of "Losers" blasted across the snow. They'd brought their own Fat Guys tape!

"You'd better turn that down!" Patti yelled from the river.

"Who's going to make me?" Wayne thundered back, turning up the heavy-metal heavyweights even louder.

"Uh, oh!" Kate said.

Oddjob had set down the block of ice he'd just finished cutting out of the river. He'd dropped the saw, too. Now the robot was swiveling around, his antennas pointing toward Wayne and Ronny and their melting snow fort.

"There he goes!" I said.

Oddjob rolled swiftly toward the thump-thump-thump of the Fat Guys. When he got to the fort he started to dance. When he'd finished flinging his arms around, there wasn't a single wall of their fort left standing!

Chapter
9

"You'll be sorry for this," Wayne shouted, glaring at us. Then he and Ronny huffed off.

Soon the judges came around. The Sleepover Friends won second prize. First prize went to a snow-and-ice dragon some high school kids made, which was sprayed all shiny with river water.

We won another trophy. It was silver, too, in the shape of a snowman. We also won another gift certificate. "Fifty dollars!" I squealed. "That jacket is in the bag!"

"I wonder if Mrs. Green has had the baby yet?" Patti said.

We decided to go over to Kate's house to dry off and celebrate our victory with some of her superfudge. When we got there the phone was ringing. It was Stephanie calling us from the hospital.

"Is it a boy?" Kate asked excitedly, holding the phone so that Patti and I could hear, too. "Or a girl?"

"Yes," Stephanie said. "And yes."

"Yes and yes?!" Kate shrieked. "Is it . . ."

"Can you believe it?" Stephanie cried. She sounded as if she wasn't sure whether to giggle or groan. "It's twins!"

Our mouths fell open. Twins! Stephanie was definitely not an only child anymore.

"My parents found out a couple of months ago," Stephanie went on. "But they didn't tell me. I guess they didn't want to spoil the surprise."

When we hung up the phone, Kate said, "There's no way we can buy *two* denim jackets! Maybe we should forget about the sled race tomorrow. We're not going to win that one, anyway."

But Patti replied firmly, "After the stuff Wayne Miller said, and poor Mark's baseball cap, we're going to win that race tomorrow, if I have to get into the harness myself!"

As I said, when Patti Jenkins decides something, watch out!

* * *

82

At twelve o'clock that night the phone rang at my house.

I fell out of bed and rushed into the hall to grab it before my parents woke up.

"Hello?" I whispered.

"It's Patti," she whispered on the other end. "Bring Bullwinkle and his harness to the starting line tomorrow at eleven. I finally thought of it!"

"Thought of what?" I asked her.

"Can't talk now — just bring him." And Patti hung up the phone.

So there Kate and I were with Bullwinkle the next morning, he in his patched red harness, the two of us with our arms around his neck, trying to calm him down. And what do Patti and Stephanie show up with? A sled, and three big grocery bags full of blue rubber balls!

"What are those for?" Kate and I said at the same time.

"What is the only command Bullwinkle obeys?" Patti asked us.

"Get your ball!" all four of us whispered at once. We didn't want to make him crazy by saying the magic word, at least not yet!

* * *

83

Bullwinkle was in doggy heaven with his head stuck inside one of the bags of balls. But it took a while for some of the other contestants to get lined up. A couple of hounds lay down with their heads where their tails should have been, and refused to move. There was a lot of biting and scratching at harnesses; there were even a few minor dogfights. So Kate and Patti and I had time to look at the Polaroid picture Stephanie had brought from the hospital to show us.

"That's Vanessa on the right, and Sting on the left," Stephanie said, with a perfectly straight face. "Or is it Sting on the right, and Vanessa. . . ."

"They actually let you name a little baby *Sting*?!" Kate screeched.

I couldn't believe it, either. I knew Stephanie's parents had been bending over backward so she wouldn't feel weird about no longer being an only child. But Sting Green was going too far — wasn't it?

Stephanie and Patti burst into giggles. "Just kidding, guys," Stephanie said. "Their names are Emma, which I chose, and Jeremy, for Nana's father, my great-grandfather." She peered more closely at the photo. "But I really *can't* tell which is which."

"You'll be able to tell them apart soon," Patti said.

The Green twins looked like a lot of babies: bald round heads, pink skin, tiny arms and plump, little legs curled up like chicken wings.

"They're cute," I said politely.

"For now, anyway," Kate added.

"All those diapers to change," Patti murmured, handing the photo back to Stephanie.

"Diapers!" Stephanie wrinkled her nose just thinking about it. "Say, Patti — maybe you could program Oddjob to . . ."

But a man wearing an orange jacket shouted, "One minute to post time!"

"Good luck!" Mark Freedman ran up to us, making the V-sign for victory. "Don't force me to give my Mets cap to that jerk Wayne, okay, Bullwinkle?" he added, patting Bullwinkle's furry head.

"Let's get ready!" Kate said.

Patti's sled looked more like a wagon, with high plastic sides. Once we'd hooked Bullwinkle to it, she got into the sled herself, and we poured the blue rubber balls in all around her.

"Planning on playing jacks?" Wayne Miller snickered as he slid by behind Killer.

But Patti had the last laugh. Way after Killer had raced off the trail after a rabbit, ignoring Wayne's shouts of "Heel! Stop! Whoooa!" Bullwinkle was chasing one blue ball after another. And Patti shot neatly across the finish line, still yelling, "Get your *ball!*"

We were waiting there for her, along with Mark Freedman and his Mets cap, Kyle Hubbard . . . , and a scowling Ronny Wallace.

Bullwinkle just stood there, panting, with a blue ball hanging out of his mouth. Kate and Stephanie and I rushed over to the sled and gave Patti a hug.

"Are you okay?" Stephanie asked her.

"My arm's a little sore from throwing, but otherwise I'm fine," she said. "How did we do?"

"You weren't first," Kate said, "but you aren't last, either. Wayne seems to have disappeared in the direction of Dannerville."

"Great race!" Mark Freedman pounded Patti on the back. "I've won an autographed baseball!"

"But we didn't win any more gift certificates for the babies," Patti said sadly.

"So we'll get two undecorated denim jackets, and decorate them ourselves!" Stephanie said, giving

Patti another squeeze. "You're supposed to be the brains here!" she added, with an eye on Ronny.

All four of us hugged and giggled and jumped up and down. And of course, Bullwinkle joined in, too!

#18 Stephanie and the Magician

"The Duvas party tomorrow afternoon," Stephanie said. "We've been canceled!"

"Canceled?!" I said. "Why?"

Stephanie looked uneasy. "Freddie decided he didn't want us," she mumbled.

"Didn't want us?" Kate squawked. "I don't believe it! What a little twerp."

"So who *does* Freddie want?" Patti asked.

"I was getting to that," Stephanie said. "Some guy named Mandrake the Magician."

"I've never heard of him," Kate said. "Who is he?"

"Nobody seems to know," Stephanie replied. "He's very mysterious. He even wears a mask. But Freddie saw Mandrake at a party and apparently that's all he's talked about ever since. He keeps going on about how Mandrake can make coins vanish into thin air and pull Coke cans out of folded newspapers, that kind of stuff.

"This is serious," Patti said. "Very serious. Little kids *love* magic. We could totally lose our audience!"

WIN FIVE NIGHTSHIRTS FOR YOUR NEXT SLEEPOVER!

SLEEPOVER FRIENDS

Enter the
SLEEPOVER FRIENDS
Super Summer Giveaway

200 Winners!

"What's your favorite thing to do at a sleepover party?"

Make your next sleepover the best ever with FIVE fabulous, oversized Sleepover Friends nightshirts for you and four friends. It's easy to win! Just tell us what's *your* favorite thing to do at a sleepover party—like telling spooky ghost stories, or doing super makeovers! Then all you have to do to enter the Sleepover Friends Super Summer Giveaway is complete the coupon below and return by November 30, 1989.

Rules: Entries must be postmarked by November 30, 1989. Winners will be picked at random from all eligible entries received. No purchase necessary. Valid only in the U.S.A. Employees of Scholastic Inc., affiliates, subsidiaries, and their families are not eligible. Void where prohibited. Winners will be notified by mail.

Fill in the coupon below or write the information on a 3″ x 5″ piece of paper and mail to: SLEEPOVER FRIENDS SUPER SUMMER GIVEAWAY, Scholastic Inc., P.O. Box 665, Cooper Station, New York, NY 10276.

Sleepover Friends Super Summer Giveaway

What's your favorite thing to do at a sleepover party?

Check one:
☐ Eating ☐ Cooking ☐ Telling Ghost Stories
☐ Makeovers ☐ Truth or Dare ☐ Other _____

Name _____ Age _____

Street _____

City, State, Zip _____

Where did you buy this *Sleepover Friends* book?
☐ Bookstore ☐ Drug Store ☐ Supermarket ☐ Other _____
☐ Book Fair ☐ Book Club ☐ Discount Store

SLE289

America's Favorite Series

THE BABY-SITTERS CLUB®

by Ann M. Martin

Collect Them All!

The seven girls at Stoneybrook Middle School get into all kinds of adventures...with school, boys, and, of course, baby-sitting!